My dearest pu

I hope this letter rea
sound. You have bee
to flee from the evil wolf Shadow.

Do not worry about me. I will hide here
until you are strong enough to return and
lead our pack. For now you must move on –
you must hide from Shadow and his spies.
If Shadow finds this letter I believe he will
try to destroy it . . .

Find a good friend – someone to help finish
my message to you. Because what I have to
say to you is important. What I have to say
is this: you must always

Please don't feel lonely. Trust in your friends
and all will be well.

Your loving mother,

Canista

Sue Bentley's books for children often include animals, fairies and wildlife. She lives in Northampton and enjoys reading, going to the cinema, relaxing by her garden pond and watching the birds feeding their babies on the lawn. At school she was always getting told off for daydreaming or staring out of the window – but she now realizes that she was storing up ideas for when she became a writer. She has met and owned many cats and dogs and each one has brought a special kind of magic to her life.

Sue Bentley

Magic Puppy

The Perfect Secret

Illustrated by *Angela Swan*

PUFFIN

To Prince – such a surprise, but so sweet-natured

PUFFIN BOOKS

Published by the Penguin Group
Penguin Books Ltd, 80 Strand, London WC2R 0RL, England
Penguin Group (USA) Inc., 375 Hudson Street, New York, New York 10014, USA
Penguin Group (Canada), 90 Eglinton Avenue East, Suite 700, Toronto, Ontario, Canada M4P 2Y3
(a division of Pearson Penguin Canada Inc.)
Penguin Ireland, 25 St Stephen's Green, Dublin 2, Ireland (a division of Penguin Books Ltd)
Penguin Group (Australia), 250 Camberwell Road, Camberwell, Victoria 3124, Australia
(a division of Pearson Australia Group Pty Ltd)
Penguin Books India Pvt Ltd, 11 Community Centre, Panchsheel Park, New Delhi – 110 017, India
Penguin Group (NZ), 67 Apollo Drive, Rosedale, North Shore 0632, New Zealand
(a division of Pearson New Zealand Ltd)
Penguin Books (South Africa) (Pty) Ltd, 24 Sturdee Avenue, Rosebank,
Johannesburg 2196, South Africa

Penguin Books Ltd, Registered Offices: 80 Strand, London WC2R 0RL, England

puffinbooks.com

First published 2009
2

Text copyright © Sue Bentley, 2009
Illustrations copyright © Angela Swan, 2009
All rights reserved

The moral right of the author and illustrator has been asserted

Set in Bembo
Made and printed in England by Clays Ltd, St Ives plc

British Library Cataloguing in Publication Data
A CIP catalogue record for this book is available from the British Library

ISBN: 978-0-141-32474-6

Prologue

The young silver-grey wolf bent his head to drink from the icy stream. It felt good to taste the water of his own world again.

Suddenly a fierce howl rang out in the night air.

'Shadow!' Storm gasped. The lone wolf who had attacked his Moon-claw pack was very close.

Storm should have known that it was

dangerous to come back. He needed to find shelter, and quickly.

There was a bright gold flash and a shower of sparks that gleamed in the moonlight. Where the young wolf had stood now crouched a tiny beagle puppy with black-and-tan fur, a white muzzle and four white socks on his sturdy little legs.

Storm hoped this disguise would protect him until he was under cover.

His tiny puppy heart beat fast. Storm's floppy rounded ears flew backwards in the cold wind as he leapt forward and tore up the hillside towards a small group of trees. The shape of a large wolf appeared above him, outlined against the star-bright sky.

'Here, my son. Hurry,' called a deep

velvety voice.

'Mother!' Storm's tailed twirled as he dashed towards her. A wriggle began at his head and worked right down his body as he yipped a greeting.

Canista licked her disguised cub's little white muzzle. 'I am pleased to see you again. You will soon be strong enough to take your place as the new leader of the Moon-claw pack. But Shadow is still looking for you.'

Storm's big midnight-blue eyes gleamed with purpose. 'Let us fight him now and force him to leave our lands forever.' He trembled at the memory of how his father and litter brothers had lost their lives to the lone wolf.

Canista took a step forward, but then bit back a cry of pain.

'You are still weak from Shadow's poisoned bite.' Storm leaned forward and huffed out a puppy breath filled with a thousand tiny gold stars. The glittery mist swirled round Canista's paw for a few seconds and then sank into her thick grey fur.

'Thank you. The pain is lessening,' she sighed gratefully. 'But there is no time to finish the healing. You must go once more to the other world. Use this disguise and return when your magic is at its full power. I will tell the other wolves to gather and await your return.'

Storm did not want to leave his mother, but he knew she was right. He nodded his tiny head.

Suddenly, another terrifying howl rang out, sounding much closer than before.

An enormous black shape appeared through the trees. The ground rang to the sound of mighty paws, which were pounding towards them.

'I know you are there, Storm. Let us finish this now!' growled a cold pitiless voice.

'Go, Storm. Save yourself!' Canista urged.

Bright gold sparks bloomed in the tiny puppy's silky-smooth black-tan-and-white fur. Storm whined as he felt the power building in his sturdy little body. The golden glow around him grew brighter. And brighter ...

Chapter
ONE

'Can you bring those flowers from the back seat with you, love?' asked Madison Berry's mum.

'OK,' Madison answered with forced brightness, making a huge effort to cheer herself up. But it didn't really work. She felt as flat as a burst balloon.

Mrs Berry let herself into the house with a spare key. 'Hello! It's only us!'

'Come right in!' Madison's gran was
wearing a light-blue tracksuit. She was
sitting in an armchair and resting her legs
on a footstool.

Madison noticed the plaster cast that
covered her right foot and reached all the

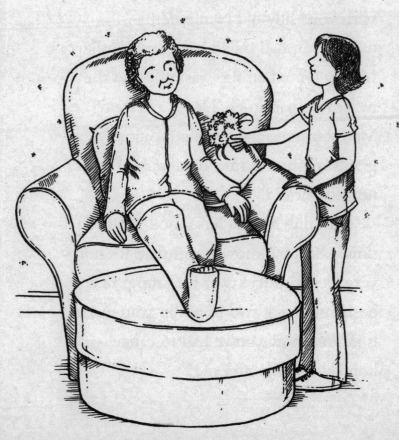

way above her knee. She went and kissed her gran's cheek and gave her the flowers.

'Aw, thanks, love. What beautiful pink roses! How's my favourite granddaughter?' she asked, smiling at Madison. 'I expect you're pretty fed up with your silly old Nanny Jen!'

Madison had called her grandmother Nanny Jen when she was little and the nickname had stuck. Despite herself, Madison managed a smile. 'Your *only* granddaughter is fine, thanks! And you're not silly or old!'

'Humph!' Nanny Jen shook her head slowly. 'I don't know about that. It's not very clever to trip over the stump of a bush and break two bones in your ankle, is it? And now you've had to cancel your holiday to look after me.'

'You couldn't help it. It was an
accident,' Madison said generously,
although she'd been looking forward
to the family holiday for months and
months. It didn't help that her two best
friends, Naomi and Shilpa, had just gone
away with Naomi's parents for a whole
month. Madison had gone away with
Naomi last year, so this year it was Shilpa's
turn.

Mrs Berry ruffled her daughter's short
dark hair approvingly. 'Thanks for being
so nice to your gran,' she whispered so
that Nanny Jen wouldn't hear, and in a
louder voice she said, 'Why don't you find
a vase to put those flowers in?'

Madison went into the kitchen and
rooted about in the cupboards. She found
a vase and filled it with water.

9

'It's going to be awkward for you in
the shower. And you'll never get up those
narrow stairs, Mum. I'm wondering if
you shouldn't just come home with us.'
Madison could hear her mum and her
gran talking in the sitting room.

'Now don't fuss, dear. I'll manage
perfectly well down here on the bed
settee. And I can ask for help if I need it.
It'll only be for a few weeks.' Nanny Jen
sighed. 'I just hope I won't get too bored
with all this sitting about.'

'I'll come and see you,' Madison
promised, coming back in with the vase
of flowers and placing it on the sideboard
next to the fish tank. She picked up a tub
of fish food. 'Shall I feed the fish for you?'

Her gran smiled broadly at her. 'Just
give them a pinch. You know that I'd

love you to visit, but I don't want you spending all your time looking after me. You make sure you get out and have some fun with your friends, won't you?'

Madison nodded. *I would if Shilpa and Naomi weren't about a million miles away*, she thought glumly. She wasn't looking forward to the next few weeks without them.

She sprinkled the flakes of food into the aquarium and then made her gran some tea, while her mum organized a shopping list. Before they left, Madison fed her gran's two budgies, Sparky and Squeak, and then helped bring some bedding downstairs and make up the bed settee.

'See you soon, Nanny Jen!' Madison sang out as she closed the front door and went out to their car.

Mrs Berry glanced across at her daughter as she drove home. 'I think I'll get your gran's shopping on the way home,' she decided. 'I know how you hate doing a big shop, so why don't you stay in the car and read? I'll be quicker doing it by myself, anyway.'

'OK. Thanks, Mum,' Madison said gratefully. She had a new *Wildlife Ways* magazine in her bag. It had brilliant pictures of colourful birds and exotic creepy crawlies. Madison was really looking forward to reading all about them. She loved anything to do with nature – even the interesting minibeasts that most other kids thought were just gross creepy-crawlies.

Her mum parked under some shady

trees at the back of the car park and went
to collect a trolley. Madison spread the
magazine open and sat flipping through
the pages for a while. Even with the
window open, the car was baking hot and
she decided to go and buy a can of cold
drink.

Madison got out of the car and had
only taken a couple of steps when there

was a flash of light from the flowers
planted round one of the trees. A whoosh
of golden sparks sprayed up into the air
and crackled as they hit the ground.

'Oh!' Dazzled, Madison blinked hard
and jumped sideways.

She rubbed her eyes and when she
could see properly again, Madison
noticed that a tiny black–and–tan puppy
with a white muzzle and four white socks
was crawling out of the flowers. It had
short legs, large rounded floppy ears and
the brightest midnight–blue eyes she had
ever seen.

Madison bent down and rubbed her
fingers together to encourage the cute
puppy to come closer and make friends.

'Hello. Where have you come from?'
she asked gently.

The puppy blinked its dewy eyes and put its head on one side. 'I have just arrived from a place that is far from here. Can you help me?' it woofed.

Chapter
TWO

Madison snatched her hand back as
if she'd been burned and looked at
the puppy in complete astonishment.
No way! She knew she had a vivid
imagination, but it must be working
overtime today. Dogs couldn't speak!

Suddenly the penny dropped. There
were obviously some kids hiding nearby,
playing a trick on her.

Madison straightened up and turned round. There were bushes dotted among the trees. She put her hands on her hips. 'OK, you can come out now!' she challenged. But no one emerged and after a few moments she looked slowly back to where the tiny puppy was blinking up at her.

'I don't get this,' she said, puzzled.

The puppy took a few steps towards her. It drew itself up. 'I am Storm of the Moon-claw pack. Who are you?' it woofed.

Madison swallowed, stunned into silence. This couldn't be happening. Talking puppies didn't just appear to ordinary girls in supermarket car parks. But this one had. Storm was looking at her quizzically, obviously expecting an answer.

'I'm M-Madison B-Berry,' she found herself stammering.

Storm bowed his head. 'I am honoured to meet you, Madison.'

'Er . . . me too. But . . . who are you? *What* are you?'

'Follow me!' Storm called, scampering past her and dashing through the trees towards a thick, spreading bush.

As Madison turned and followed the tiny puppy, there was another bright golden flash. She looked for him but he had disappeared and in his place beside the bush crouched a magnificent young silver-grey wolf with glowing midnight-blue eyes. Gold sparks glimmered like jewels in the thick ruff round its neck.

Madison gasped, eyeing the wolf's powerful muscles and sharp teeth. 'Storm?'

'Yes, it is me, Madison. Do not be afraid,' Storm said in a deep velvety growl.

Before Madison could get used to the incredible young wolf there was a final dazzling flash of gold light and Storm was once again a silky-smooth black-and-tan puppy with four little white socks.

'Wow! That's amazing. No one would know that you're a wolf,' Madison exclaimed. 'But why are you in hiding?'

Storm began to tremble all over and his
eyes narrowed with anger and fear. 'The
fierce lone wolf, who killed my father
and litter brothers and left my mother
wounded, is looking for me. He is called
Shadow. Can you help me, Madison?'

'Of course I will!' Madison's heart went
out to him. Storm was totally stunning as

a young wolf, but as a helpless puppy he was adorable. She bent down to pick him up and then walked back through the trees and on to the car park.

'I'm going to ask my mum if I can keep you,' she crooned, kissing the top of his soft little head and enjoying his clean puppy smell.

'Keep who? What have you got there?' asked a voice at her side.

Madison whirled round to see her mum approaching. She'd been so busy cuddling Storm that she hadn't noticed her trundling the shopping towards the car.

'I've just found him. Isn't he gorgeous? He's called Storm and he can ta—' Madison began, but suddenly Storm reached up and tapped her cheek with a tiny white-tipped front paw.

'Wrr-rrr-uu-ff!' he wailed loudly, looking up at her with pleading deep-blue eyes and shaking his head.

Madison looked down at Storm in confusion, before it dawned on her that Storm didn't want her to tell her mum about him. She patted him reassuringly, letting him know that she understood, before looking back up at her mum. 'I . . . um, think Storm's a stray. Can we take him home and look after him?' she asked.

'Storm? You've already given him a name? He's rather cute, isn't he? But he was just making a strange noise as if there's something wrong with him. The poor mite probably needs to be taken to a vet.'

'No! He doesn't. He's fine!' Madison

burst out. 'I mean . . . that funny noise he made was . . . a sneeze. Um . . . because of . . . the car fumes,' she said in a burst of inspiration.

Her mum looked more closely at Storm. She stroked his little head. 'He certainly looks healthy enough. You might be right about the fumes. But we can't just take him home. What if he belongs to someone who's inside the store?'

Madison thought quickly. 'I'll go inside and ask if anyone's reported a lost puppy.' Before her mum had a chance to protest, she ran across the car park. Holding Storm carefully, she went through the automatic entrance doors and hurried towards the customer service desk.

A smart woman in a crisp blue-and-white uniform frowned at her. 'I'm afraid you can't bring that puppy in here, young lady. No animals are allowed.'

'Oh, sorry,' Madison said, pretending that she wasn't aware of the rules.

She moved slowly away from the desk and timed it so that she met her mum coming in through the automatic doors. 'No one's reported a lost puppy,' she said, taking her mum's arm and gently steering her back out. *It wasn't exactly a fib*, she thought, *since I didn't even ask about one.* 'So can we look after Storm? I'll do everything for him: take him for walks, feed him, wipe up muddy paw prints, bath him.'

Her mum sighed. 'It's not really a good time. We've got your gran to look after and I for one don't fancy the complications of puppy puddles and chewed slippers.'

Storm gave an indignant little woof at the very idea that he might not be fully house-trained.

Madison had to try hard not to grin. She forced herself to look serious again.

'Oh, please, Mum. Please, please,' she begged. 'Look how cute he is. He'll take up hardly any room. And Nanny Jen will love Storm. You know how she is about animals. And she's all fed up about her poorly ankle and she can't go out much. I bet it'll cheer her up loads to have a puppy to cuddle,' she rushed on.

'Enough already!' Her mum held up her hands. 'I suppose we could give it a try. But I don't know what your dad's going to say when he sees him.'

'He'll love him to bits, like I do!'

Mrs Berry smiled. 'You're probably right at that. You do realize that I'm going to have to report Storm as a stray? If someone comes forward to claim him, there'll be no arguments. OK?'

'It's a deal!' Madison agreed readily,

positive that no one was going to come calling for her new little friend. Before she'd met Storm she'd been feeling really down in the dumps about their cancelled holiday and having no friends to hang out with. But the long, lonely weeks ahead were starting to look a bit brighter already.

Chapter
THREE

'You must be hungry after your long journey,' Madison said, forking dog food into a bowl.

Storm licked his lips eagerly. The moment she put the bowl on to the kitchen floor, he bounded forward and began chomping the food.

Madison watched him, smiling. It was still hard to believe that this magic puppy had chosen her to be his friend.

Storm finished eating and sat licking his chops, while Madison washed his dish and put it away.

'He soon polished that off!' Madison's mum said from over by the kitchen counter where she was making supper.

'I'll take him upstairs to show him where he'll be sleeping,' Madison said

happily. 'Come on, Storm. Let's go!' she called.

Storm immediately jumped to his feet and scampered across the kitchen towards her.

Mrs Berry watched them. 'That puppy seems to know exactly what you're saying,' she commented.

Madison smiled to herself. If only her mum knew!

'I'm sorry that I almost gave away your secret to Mum earlier,' she whispered to Storm as they climbed the stairs.

'I do not think she noticed. Grown-up humans seem to find it hard to believe in magic,' he woofed. His furry brow creased as he looked serious. 'You must never tell anyone my secret. Promise me, Madison.'

'Oh,' Madison said, disappointed. She

had been hoping that she could share her wonderful news with Nanny Jen, who was brilliant at keeping secrets. But she was prepared to do anything to help keep the tiny puppy safe. 'OK then. Cross my heart. No one's going to hear about you from me. You're safe with me.'

Storm looked up at her, his deep-blue eyes shining. 'Thank you, Madison.'

In her bedroom, Madison spread a piece of old blanket on top of her duvet. She patted it encouragingly. 'Mum says you have to sleep on this because she doesn't want puppy hairs all over the bed. But I don't mind them. You can sleep next to me when we're by ourselves.'

Storm sprang up on to the bed, leaving a shower of faint gold sparks in the air behind him.

'Wow! Isn't that a dead giveaway?'
Madison asked, eyeing the glittery trail. 'I
mean – someone's going to notice if little
sparks fly off you all the time, aren't they?'

'I will use my magic, so that only you
can see and hear me properly,' the puppy
woofed. 'Other humans will think I am
an ordinary puppy.'

'You can do that? Cool! That makes
things much easier,' Madison said
delightedly.

Storm sniffed at the blanket and then
scrabbled it into messy folds, before
turning round in circles and lying
down. 'This is a safe place!' he sighed
contentedly.

Madison sat down beside him. 'I'm
glad you like it, because I love having you
living with me.'

She stroked the little pup as she stared
idly out of her bedroom window. It
overlooked a large area of overgrown
land, which reached down to the river.
A huge factory used to stand on the site,
but it had been pulled down ages ago.

Clumps of waist-high nettles and
brambles covered with starry-white
flowers sprawled everywhere. Bushes and
tall weeds had sprouted up around the
trees, turning the field into a mini-jungle.

Storm sat up and craned his neck to

look for movements in the long grass
and Madison saw his eyes gleam and his
floppy ears twitch with sudden interest.

'Rabbits!' he yapped.

'Yes. I sometimes borrow Dad's
binoculars to watch them. There are lots
of birds and butterflies too and I even
saw a fox once. There's a gap in the fence
that no one's bothered to repair and lots
of people take their dogs for walks there.
Would you like to go over?'

Storm leapt to his feet again, his whole
body quivering with eagerness. 'Walking
is my favourite thing!'

Madison smiled. 'Come on then. I'll
just go and tell Mum where we're going.
We can't be long because Dad will be
home soon and we'll be having supper.'

*

Madison went outside with Storm at her heels. They were walking the few metres to the gap in the fence when a dark-green jeep drew up. A fair-haired man wearing green combats, walking boots and a waistcoat with lots of pockets got out and opened the boot.

He nodded and smiled at Madison and Storm. 'Hello there, young lady. Cute puppy!' he said, unloading a rucksack and a camera.

Madison smiled back at him, before he went into the field.

She noticed that there were lots of colourful stickers with badgers, birds and insects on them in the jeep's back window. *He must be really keen on wildlife*, she thought.

Madison stepped through the gap in the fence and Storm followed her. He gave an eager little woof and dived beneath a tangle of grass and leaves. As he weaved about, trying to sniff out rabbit trails, Madison could just see the white tip of his jaunty little tail poking into the air. At one point he disturbed a wood pigeon.

It rose up from a bush with a noisy clatter of wings.

'Yipe!' Storm skittered sideways with his tail between his legs.

Madison grinned at his antics. She walked on, leaving him to explore and run off some energy. They didn't see the man from the jeep again, and Madison assumed that he was birdwatching.

Time was getting on and she decided to double-back and head for home.

'Storm! Come here, boy! Let's go!'

Storm came hurtling towards her with his tongue hanging out and his floppy ears flying out behind him. There were greenish streaks of something nasty all over him. As he reached her she got a pungent whiff.

'Yuck! You smell terrible,' she groaned.

'Mum will go bonkers when she sees the state you're in. I'm going to have to smuggle you up to the bathroom.'

Storm's small white teeth flashed in a doggy grin. 'I like the interesting smells on my fur. But I will roll in the grass to get myself clean!' he woofed.

Madison couldn't help laughing. 'Trust me. That's *not* going to work.'

Chapter
FOUR

Mr Berry was in the hall when Madison
and Storm came downstairs together. He
had changed out of his work suit into
jeans and a polo shirt.

'Hi, Madison. Hello, little fella! I've
just been hearing all about you,' he said,
bending down to scratch Storm under
the chin. 'It's going to be nice to have a
puppy around the place.'

Madison was relieved that her dad hadn't made a big deal about her new friend. Her mum must have filled him in with all the details. Storm wagged his tail and he licked Mr Berry's fingers, enjoying all the fuss.

'What's that smell? Have you been using that expensive shower gel I bought for your mum's birthday, Madison?' her dad said suspiciously, looking up at her.

'What me? No way,' Madison said innocently. *But Storm has!*

'Supper's on the table!' her mum called from the kitchen, which saved her from answering more questions.

'Great! I'm starving.' Madison quickly scooped up Storm and shot into the kitchen with him. She put the puppy down and he curled up sleepily under the

table, with his head resting on her feet.

Madison heaped food on to her plate. As they ate, she told her mum and dad about the man in the jeep. 'He seemed to have a lot of camera equipment.'

Mrs Berry looked interested. 'Perhaps someone's finally going to do something about that land. It's a terrible eyesore. It's so overgrown and there are always letters in the local paper about kids hanging around and being a nuisance. I'd rather some smart new houses were built there.'

'I like it how it is. It's good for wildlife,' Madison said.

'Animals always come first with you, don't they?' her dad said, smiling. 'You're just like your gran. She spent a fortune on that posh budgie cage for Sparky and Squeak and I've lost count of the number of bird feeders in her garden.' He turned to his wife. 'How was Mum today? Is she coping with that cast on her leg?'

Madison's mum told him all about their visit earlier. 'Her only worry is that she'll get bored. Madison and I will pop over to see her tomorrow and take her shopping.'

'Aren't you forgetting someone?' Madison asked. 'Storm! Nanny Jen will be so surprised when she sees that I've got a new puppy.'

Her mum and dad laughed. 'I expect she will,' her dad agreed.

After they'd finished eating, Madison helped clear away the dishes and went into the sitting room with Storm. 'There's a brilliant programme about deep-sea creatures just starting,' she told him.

'Sounds good. I'll watch it with you,' her dad said.

Madison realized that she had spoken louder than she'd meant to. She'd have to be more careful about keeping Storm's secret.

Madison sat on the sofa next to her dad and settled Storm on her lap. He seemed fascinated by the weird-looking fishes with huge eyes and long curved teeth that loomed out of the inky darkness of the ocean depths.

'Aren't they amazing?' Madison said.
'Like creatures from another planet!'

'I must say that you're very cheerful
for someone who's just had their holiday
cancelled and who was saying how much
she was missing her two best friends,' her
dad commented.

A pang of guilt rose up inside Madison.
She'd hardly given Shilpa and Naomi

a thought over the last few hours. She wasn't missing them nearly as much now that she had a new furry friend. She shrugged, stroking Storm's silky ears. 'It's no use stressing over stuff you can't change, is it?' she said thoughtfully.

After the TV programme finished, Madison took Storm upstairs, planning to relax with him and finish reading her wildlife magazine. But Storm seemed to have other ideas. He scampered across the room and leapt on to a chair near the window. He stood up on his short back legs and put his front paws on the window sill.

'What are you looking at?' Madison asked, going over to stand beside him. 'The place down there that was full of exciting smells,' he woofed, looking up at

her hopefully with big eyes and wagging his tail.

'I'll take you over there again tomorrow morning,' she promised. 'Oh, look. There's that man we saw earlier.'

The fair-haired man in green combats was stepping out of the gap in the fence.

'He's been over there for ages,' Madison said, hoping as hard as she could that it wasn't anything to do with the houses that her mum had said might be built on the land.

Madison stroked Storm's silky ears as they watched him load his equipment in the jeep, before driving away.

Chapter
FIVE

The following morning, Madison woke bright and early to find sunshine pouring through a crack in the curtains. There was a warm weight on one arm. She smiled and reached out to stroke Storm, who was cuddled up close to her.

'Did you sleep well?' she asked him.

'Very well, thank you,' Storm woofed politely. He stood up and gave himself a shake. 'I am ready for a walk now!'

Smiling at his eagerness, Madison jumped out of bed and threw on some jeans, a T-shirt and trainers. She could hear movements in the bathroom as her dad got ready for work.

She fed Storm in the kitchen and was hastily cramming toast into her mouth

when her dad came in.

'Slow down, Madison! Where's the fire?' he teased.

'Storm said that he wants to –' Madison stopped. 'I mean, I want to take Storm for a walk in the field before Mum and I go to Nanny Jen's,' she quickly corrected.

Luckily, her dad was searching his pockets for his car keys and didn't notice.

'Have a good day at work! Laters!' she called out as she rushed out of the kitchen and headed towards the front door, with Storm gambolling after her.

As they walked down the street, Madison noticed that the green jeep was parked there again. There was no sign of the man so she assumed he must be birdwatching in the field again.

Madison noticed a girl, who looked

about twelve years old, coming down the street towards them. She had a friendly face and her blonde hair was tied back in a ponytail.

'Hi!' the girl said, pausing as she drew level. 'Do you live around here? I wondered if you knew where the nearest food shop is.'

'I live just up the road. There's a garage just round the corner,' Madison said helpfully. 'It sells sandwiches and stuff.'

'Oh, right. Thanks. I'm Ellie Robertson, by the way,' the girl said.

'Hi, Ellie. I'm Madison.'

Ellie smiled. 'Your puppy's gorgeous. What's his name?'

'Storm,' Madison told her.

Storm wagged his tail and looked up at Ellie.

The older girl bent down to stroke the
tiny puppy. 'I love dogs. Storm doesn't
look very old. Have you had him long?
I don't think I've ever seen a puppy with
such amazing big blue eyes.'

'Me neither. Storm's one of a kind. I've
only just got him,' Madison said fondly.

'I haven't seen you round here before,'
she said, changing the subject before Ellie
asked any awkward questions.

'I'm here with my dad. He's a naturalist.
That's our car,' Ellie said, pointing towards
the jeep. 'I'm helping Dad right now
since it's the school holidays. He never
thinks of food when he's working, but
he'll want lunch later and expect me to
produce some by magic!'

Madison knew that a naturalist was
someone who studies animals and plants.
It was something she'd love to do when
she grew up. 'Are you looking at birds?
We get lots in the field.'

Ellie shook her head. 'Dad's special
interest is small mammals. He thinks there
could be dormice in the field.'

'Oh, wow!' Madison said excitedly.

'Dormice are really rare, aren't they?
They're so cute with those ginger coats,
pink noses and big fluffy tails. They look
more like tiny hamsters than mice.'

'Yeah, they are,' Ellie said, looking
surprised. 'You seem to know all about
them.'

'I don't really,' Madison admitted.
'I've seen pictures and read a bit about
dormice being endangered. I'd love
to get a close look at a real one.' She
remembered something else she'd read.
'Don't you have to have a special licence
to handle them?'

Ellie nodded. 'That's right. Dad has one.
Why don't you come over and see how
we're doing later? Dad won't mind.'

'I'd love to!' Madison said.

'OK then. I'd better get those

sandwiches. Bye! Bye, Storm,' Ellie said, giving him a gentle pat.

Madison waved as Ellie walked away. 'She seemed really nice, didn't she?'

Storm nodded. 'I liked her too.'

Madison and Storm continued on their way to the field. They were almost there when three boys, holding cans of drink, burst out of the gap in the fence. Madison recognized them from school. They were

two years above her and were always
being a nuisance and picking on smaller
kids.

She felt herself tensing as the boys
scrunched up the cans and began kicking
them about. Laughing and jostling each
other, they booted a can in her direction.

It bounced very close to Storm. He
yapped in surprise and had to skitter
sideways to avoid being struck.

'Hey, watch it!' Madison cried
protectively.

One of the boys frowned. He was small
and stocky and there was a mean look
on his face. 'Who do you think you are,
telling us what to do?' he challenged.

Madison took a step backwards as the
tough boy nudged his friends. They spread
out across the path barring her way.

'Excuse me. I . . . I want to get to the field,' she said, her heart thumping.

'Tough! You'll have to go round the block, won't you?' the stocky boy sneered.

Madison gulped, wondering whether to risk walking towards the three of them in the hope that they'd let her through. But the boys folded their arms and stood their ground.

Storm growled softly.

Madison felt a peculiar warm tingling sensation flow down her spine as large gold sparks ignited in Storm's smooth fur and his broad floppy ears crackled and fizzed with miniature lightning bolts.

Something very strange was about to happen.

Chapter
SIX

Madison watched in complete
amazement as Storm raised a white-
tipped front paw and a shower of sparks
whooshed out and turned into a cloud of
tiny flies. They whirled round the boys,
buzzing annoyingly, getting into their hair
and crawling on their skin.

'Argh!' the boys yelled, batting their
hands and hopping about.

'Where did they come from?'

'Yuck! I just swallowed one!' the stocky
boy complained.

'I think I've got one in my pants!'
yelled his mate, capering about.

Madison started laughing as the boys
tore down the street pursued by the cloud
of itchy flies and disappeared round the
corner. 'You are so bad, Storm! But it
served those bullies right!'

Storm grinned cheekily as every last
golden spark faded from his fur. 'I am glad

that I could help!'

Madison stepped into the field and Storm followed her. They took one of the narrow pathways that wove through the long grass. 'Don't get all muddy again,' she warned him. 'We're going straight over to my gran's house when we get back and I haven't got time to give you another bath.'

At the word 'bath', Storm wrinkled his nose. He was careful to avoid any ditches and instead, rooted out a mossy old stick. Madison grinned as he ambled along with it proudly grasped in his mouth.

Madison spotted Ellie and her dad with a camera and tripod near a patch of brambles in the distance. Ellie saw her looking and waved.

Madison was really tempted to jog over

and see what they were doing, but she decided that she'd better go home. Her mum would be impatient to leave and Nanny Jen was expecting them.

She looked down at Storm. 'We can come back again tomorrow. I'd love it if Ellie's dad found dormice.'

'Goodness me!' Nanny Jen exclaimed delightedly, the moment Madison walked in with Storm in her arms. 'You didn't say anything about having a new puppy when you left yesterday! Where did he come from?'

You wouldn't believe me if I told you, Madison thought.

She put Storm on the settee and then explained about finding him in the supermarket car park. 'I knew you'd like him. I already love Storm to bits.'

'I can see why. He's irresistible.' Nanny
Jen's eyes softened as Storm stepped
carefully on to her lap and curled into a
ball. She stroked his silky-smooth fur.
'A dog's such a wonderful companion,'
she said quietly.

Madison thought her gran sounded
rather sad. It had been a long time since
Grandad had died. She knew that despite

their regular family visits, Nanny Jen
sometimes got lonely, although she didn't
like to admit it.

Madison had a sudden idea. 'I know!
Why don't *you* get a puppy?' she said
eagerly.

Storm wagged his tail and gave a woof
of agreement.

'Me?' Nanny Jen said, frowning.
'I wouldn't know where to start looking
for one!'

'That's easy-peasy,' Madison said. 'Lots
of dogs need homes. You just phone up
the animal rescue centre –'

'Now Madison, don't go running
away with yourself,' Mrs Berry warned
as she came in from the kitchen with
a sandwich and a drink on a tray. 'Your
gran's ankle's going to take at least two

months to mend. The last thing she wants is an energetic new puppy.'

'But I could help her train it and take it for walks with Storm. And it would cheer her up and . . .' As her mum raised her eyebrows, Madison trailed off. 'OK – bad idea,' she sighed.

Nanny Jen winked at Madison and reached out to squeeze her hand. There was a rebellious spark in her eye. 'I'll think about what you said,' she said softly. 'Anyway, what have you been doing, apart from having fun with Storm?'

'Well – we just met a really nice girl called Ellie. She's helping her dad look for dormice in the field next to our house,' Madison explained.

'Dormice? I used to see those quite a lot when I was a girl.' Nanny Jen said. 'We had cornfields and hedgerows at the back of our cottage. It's hard to imagine that the little creatures are endangered now.'

'Yes, it's really sad. But wouldn't it be brilliant if there *are* dormice in our field? That would make it a really special place,' Madison enthused.

'Well, I'm not keen about having a load of mice scurrying about,' Mrs Berry said, shuddering. 'They might infest our house

when their food starts running out in the winter.'

'Mu-um! They wouldn't. They're not that sort of mouse,' Madison protested. 'And, anyway, dormice hibernate, so they don't need any winter food.'

'Quite right,' her gran agreed. 'And I don't know why's there's so much fuss in the papers about that field being an eyesore. Wildlife has to live somewhere. We need to make room for it in this hectic world.'

Madison couldn't have agreed more. She felt a stir of affection for Nanny Jen.

While her gran ate her lunch, Madison helped put away the shopping and then pegged out some washing in the garden. Soon afterwards, they said their goodbyes and left, but not before Nanny Jen insisted on giving Storm a final cuddle.

'You come and see me again, very soon,' she said to him.

Storm woofed softly in answer, and licked the end of her nose with his little pink tongue.

Chapter
SEVEN

Saturday dawned bright and clear. The
moment breakfast was over Madison
dashed out of the house, with Storm
scampering after her, and headed for the
field. 'I wonder how Ellie and her dad
are getting on. I can't wait to see my
first ever real live dormouse!' she said
enthusiastically.

'I would like to see one too. I do not

think we have them in my home world,'
Storm yapped.

Madison tried to imagine what a
wintry world ruled by magnificent wolves
was like. She thought of sunlight glinting
on a vast frozen landscape of mountains,
lakes and forests. It must be cold and
beautiful and very dangerous.

'Uh-oh.' Madison spotted the three
tough boys at the end of her street. They
all held sticks and were running them
along some railings to make a clattering
noise. Luckily, the boys disappeared round
the corner without seeing them.

Madison and Storm quickly slipped
through the fence and went looking for
Ellie and her dad. Storm snuffled along,
head down and tail up. They rounded a
huge tangled clump of brambles and

came upon Ellie writing in a notebook.

'Hi! How's it going?' Madison asked.

Ellie looked up and smiled. 'Hi! We've
made some progress. Come and have a
look.' She led the way to where her dad
had set up his camera and tripod. His
canvas bag was open on the ground. 'Dad,

this is Madison, who I told you about.
You met her the other day.'

Mr Robertson smiled. 'Hello, Madison.
I remember. And this must be Storm.'

Storm blinked up at him and wagged
his tail. 'Grr-uf!'

'Hello, Mr Robertson,' Madison said
politely.

'Call me Oliver. Everyone does.'

'Can we show Madison what we've
found?' Ellie asked, reaching into his bag
and bringing out a small cardboard box.

Madison bent close as Ellie opened the
flap. Inside the box was a rather untidy
and loosely woven nest, made of stripped
stems, grass and bramble leaves. 'Was there
anything inside?' she asked hopefully.

Oliver shook his head. 'We found
this on the ground, where it had been

knocked or fallen down. It's a summer breeding nest and it's quite fresh so it's probably in use. Unfortunately, there were some lads over here earlier, messing about and bashing things down with sticks.'

'Dad asked them to be careful, but they just gave him a mouthful of cheek,' Ellie put in crossly.

Madison didn't need three guesses to

know who the boys were. 'Did you say a breeding nest? So ... where are the babies?' she asked worriedly.

'They're probably safe. The female dormouse usually builds more than one nest. If she's severely disturbed, she'll move her young to one of the others.'

'Oh good,' Madison said, relieved.

Storm reared up and poked his head forward to look into the box. He sniffed at it, his tail wagging interestedly.

'Getting the scent are you, little fella?' Oliver smiled and stroked the tiny puppy's floppy ears. He turned back to Madison. 'At least we're pretty sure now that dormice are around. But we need to find more nests before we can be certain there's a healthy breeding colony here.'

'We're going to do a night watch

tomorrow,' Ellie told her. 'Dormice are
more active then and we've got a better
chance of seeing them.'

'Can we come and help?' Madison
asked eagerly.

Oliver smiled. 'Any extra help's always
welcome. But I'm not sure that it's a good
idea to bring Storm. If he starts barking
and getting overexcited, he'll ruin our
chances of seeing any dormice.'

'Storm would never do that. He's very
well trained,' Madison assured him, but
she could see that Oliver still looked
doubtful. 'I'll show you,' she said on
impulse. 'Sit!' she ordered, hoping Storm
got the message.

Storm blinked at her in surprise, but
obediently sat down.

'Good boy. Now, stay,' Madison said

firmly. She turned her back and walked about four metres away, keeping her fingers crossed.

Storm didn't run after her. He stayed put, as if waiting for another command.

Madison turned round and walked back towards him. She stopped in front of him and lifted her hand. To her amazement Storm stood up, wove neatly round her legs and sat down at heel with his tail tucked beneath him.

'Wow! You two are great. How many hours at puppy training classes did that take?' asked Ellie.

'Oh . . . um, not as many you might think,' Madison said vaguely.

'I guess we'll see you *and* Storm, tomorrow night then,' Oliver said.

'You bet!' Madison said, grinning as she moved away. 'That was impressive,' she whispered to Storm when they were out of earshot. 'How did you know what to do?'

Storm put his head on one side as he looked at her. 'I have seen pet dogs act like that with their humans. I just copied them!'

Madison planned to walk over and visit her gran the following afternoon. The phone rang just as they were about to set off. It was Nanny Jen.

'I'm glad I caught you. I wondered if you'd mind popping into the pet shop for me?' she asked. 'I've almost run out of budgie seed.'

'No problem,' Madison told her.

She loved the pet shop with its warm, musty smell, tanks of tropical fish and cages full of small birds, hamsters and gerbils. Madison and Storm spent some time looking around, before buying seed for Sparky and Squeak and a soft ball and some dog chews for Storm.

At her gran's house Madison fed the budgies and then suggested they all go out into the garden so Storm could play with his new ball. Nanny Jen hobbled outside with her walking frame and sat in

a garden chair.

Storm enjoyed a lively game of fetch.
Nanny Jen and Madison took it in turns
to throw the ball for him and he raced
around after it with his pink tongue
hanging out. Afterwards he flopped on to
the lawn, panting.

Nanny Jen enjoyed the cheeky pup's antics. 'You two are better than a tonic! You really cheer me up.' She looked quizzically at Madison. 'Did you mean it about helping me to look after a new puppy and taking it for walks?'

Madison did a double take. 'Definitely! So – does that mean you're getting one? When is it –'

'Calm down, love. Nothing's decided yet,' her gran interrupted kindly.

Madison sighed. Why did grown-ups always take so long making their minds up about things?

'Shall I water your veggies for you?' she said, turning on the outside tap and hauling the hose across the lawn.

As a stream of water splashed out, Storm made an amazing recovery and jumped to his feet. Bouncing down on to his front legs, he waggled his tiny rear-end. He pounced on the hose, barking and snapping at the stream of water.

'You're a clown!' Madison whispered affectionately so that Nanny Jen couldn't hear. 'I hope you can stay with me forever and ever.'

A serious expression crossed Storm's little face. He sat down and looked up at her. 'I cannot do that. One day I must return to my homeland and the Moon-claw pack. Do you understand that, Madison?'

'Um . . . yes. But that won't be for ages yet, will it?' she asked hopefully.

'I do not know,' Storm admitted. 'But if Shadow finds me, I may have to leave suddenly without saying goodbye.'

Madison felt a sharp pang as she knew
that she'd never be ready to lose her furry
friend. She pushed the uncomfortable
idea to the back of her mind and made a
firm promise with herself to enjoy every
single moment with Storm.

Chapter
EIGHT

As the sun went down the evening sky was painted in glorious shades of orange, pink and violet. Madison glanced out of the kitchen window, watching as the first stars appeared.

'I'm not sure it's a good idea for you to go crawling round that field in the dark all by yourself,' Madison's mum said doubtfully as she finished unloading the dishwasher.

'But I'll be with Storm!' Madison protested. 'And Ellie and her dad will be there. I'll be fine!'

'I think your mum's right,' her dad said, coming into the kitchen. 'It's too dangerous. You could easily stumble into a ditch and hurt yourself. I'll come with you. I'll just go and change my shoes.'

'Oh great!' Madison complained to Storm as her mum and dad both went into the hall. 'They still think I'm about four instead of nearly nine years old.'

Storm's ears twitched and he gave a shrill whine and began pawing frantically at the back door. Madison opened it for him automatically, still feeling grumpy about having to trail her dad along like a little kid.

It was a moment before she realized
that a loud snapping and growling noise
was coming from outside the front of the
house.

She ran into the sitting room and
peered out of the window. A man
struggling with two large dogs on leads
was walking beneath a street light.
Madison saw that the dogs seemed to
have wolf-like pale eyes and extra large
teeth. They were straining to get into the

front garden. The man managed to get them under control and shut them in the back of a nearby car before driving off.

Madison shivered. Those dogs gave her a very bad feeling.

A horrible suspicion crept over her as she remembered what Storm had said to her at Nanny Jen's earlier about having to leave suddenly if Shadow found him.

Shadow had sent those dogs!

Somehow, Madison knew that she was right. Storm must have heard them growling at the front of the house and rushed outside to hide. Her heart was in her mouth as she ran into the back garden.

'Storm! Where are you?' she whispered. 'You're safe. You can come out now!'

But however much Madison called, he

didn't answer. A guilty feeling rose in her chest. Why hadn't she paid more attention when he'd pawed at the back door?

What if Storm had gone? It was unbearable to think that she would never see her puppy friend again.

After carefully checking the back garden and finding no sign of Storm, Madison raced round the side of the house. She emerged into the street just in time to catch sight of a small dark shape speeding headlong towards the gap in the fence. Four little white socks gleamed in moonlight.

Madison's heart leapt with relief. 'Storm!'

She shot after the terrified puppy without a second thought. Reaching the fence, she stumbled through the gap. Too

far away now from street lights, she stood
blinking, her eyes trying to adjust to the
sudden darkness. She could barely see half
a metre in front of her, but there was no
time to run back home for a torch.

'Storm! It's me. Where are you?' she
called.

Twigs snapped under her feet and there
were rustling noises in the nearby bushes
as Madison pushed ahead. She narrowly
avoided running into a tree. Lurching to
one side, she almost went sprawling as her
foot disappeared down a hole.

'Ow!' Thrown off balance she fell
sideways, wrenching her leg. Pain shot
through her knee, making her gasp, but
she ignored it and limped forward.

Branches tugged at Madison's hair and
brushed against her face as she pressed on

blindly. Brambles and tall thistles loomed
out of the darkness. The familiar field
now seemed strange and menacing.

Madison stopped, panting. Even the
faint light from the gap in the fence had
disappeared and she couldn't tell which
direction she was facing.

'Storm!' she whispered desperately.
'Shadow's dogs have gone. You're safe
now. Please, come out!'

Madison heard a faint whimper and a
tingling feeling crept down her spine.
A tiny light appeared, which grew
brighter as Storm crawled out from
behind an old log and came towards her.
His whole body was glowing softly like
a lantern and spreading golden light in a
metre-wide circle.

'Oh, thank goodness!' Madison

breathed as she swept him up and
wrapped her arms round him. She could
feel his tiny heart beating against her
palms. 'I'm really sorry. I was so busy
thinking about myself back there that
I didn't realize you were in danger,' she
apologized, swallowing guilty tears.

Storm licked her chin with his warm
tongue. 'It does not matter. You came here
by yourself to find me. You were very brave.'

'I wasn't really. I'm just glad you're all right. I couldn't bear anything to happen to you. Oh!' Madison gasped as a fresh wave of pain stabbed at her knee. Now that she had found Storm, she felt sick and her legs had gone all wobbly.

'You are hurt, Madison. I will make you better.'

Storm huffed out a warm breath that glinted with a thousand tiny gold stars. The sparkly mist swirled round Madison's knee for a few seconds before it sank into her jeans and disappeared. The pain grew hot and sharp for a moment, but then began to ebb away just as if it had gone out with the tide at the seashore.

'Thanks, Storm. I'm fine now,' she whispered gratefully, reaching out to pick him up. 'Maybe we'd better go back home and get a torch. I don't know whether Ellie and Oliver are here yet, I wasn't exactly looking for their jeep when I ran after you. Oh heck – Dad!' she gasped, remembering that he was supposed to be coming with her and would probably be wondering where she'd got to.

She was about to ask Storm to help her find the way back through the darkness, when a bloodcurdling cry rang out. Twigs snapped and branches cracked as two shadowy fingers leapt out of the bushes. There was thud as a third figure jumped down from a tree.

A hand grabbed her arm. 'Don't move!' a rough voice ordered.

Chapter
NINE

Madison cried out in alarm. She clutched
Storm against her. Was this another of
Shadow's attacks? Her pulses raced at the
thought of facing Storm's fierce enemy.

'This is our den and you're trespassing!'
another voice yelled.

Beams of torchlight lit up three familiar
faces streaked with brown and green paint
beneath green-patterned camouflage

bandanas. It was the three older boys from Madison's school.

Relief swept through Madison. Her fear faded and suddenly she was angrier than she had ever been in her life.

'You stupid, stupid muppets!' she raged. 'Why don't you lot act your age? I almost fainted with fright!'

'Who are you calling a muppet?' asked the small stocky boy, who seemed to be the ringleader.

'What are we going to do with her, Guy?' another boy asked.

'Take her prisoner,' Guy said. 'And grab that soppy-looking puppy she's holding. We'll tie it to that log.'

'I wouldn't try that, if I were you!' Madison warned.

'Yeah! Are you gonna stop me?'

Storm's lip curled as he showed his teeth at the boys. 'Put me down, Madison,' he growled softly.

Madison quickly yanked her arm free, bent down and did as he asked. Storm vanished instantly into the shadows.

'Hey! Where did that mangy mutt go?' one of the boys said.

'Forget it. Grab her!' Guy ordered.

Madison folded her arms and calmly faced the three boys. They paused in

surprise, obviously expecting her to
try and run. She felt a strong prickling
sensation down her spine and heard a
faint crackling of magical sparks from one
of the bushes.

'One, two . . . three,' she counted.

Whoosh! A mini-tornado of grass and
leaves rose into the air. It whirled towards
the boys, forging a pathway through the
weedy grass. *Swirl!* It knocked them off
their feet. Three stunned faces gazed at
Madison as they whizzed round and
round, in a dizzy twirl as if they were in
a tumble dryer. *Splop!* The tornado spat
them out, scattered them on their backs
and dumped a blanket of leafy grass all
over them.

Quick as a flash, Madison picked up
the boys' torches, which they'd dropped

in their confusion.

'Oo-er! I feel sick,' Guy moaned, holding his head and spitting out a bit of leaf. He looked pale under his face paint. 'What just happened?'

'Who cares? I'm legging it!' cried his friend.

'Me too! This place is haunted!' the other yelled.

Madison took pity on them and swung the torches round, until she could see the fence. It wasn't very far away at all and she realized that she must have been running in circles while searching for Storm.

'This way!' The boys weaved about unsteadily as they stumbled towards the exit.

'Wait for me!' Guy bleated in a wobbly voice as he squeezed through the fence.

The sound of retreating footsteps faded from the street outside

Laughter bubbled up inside Madison as she turned back to Storm. He padded towards her, the last few golden sparks fading from his fur. 'That'll teach them to mess with us!' she said.

Just then, a tall figure appeared at the gap in the fence.

'Here's Oliver and Ellie now!' Madison guessed, lifting the torch. She started to smile but the grin froze on her face.

Her dad stood there, wearing a furious expression in the torchlight.

Madison's heart sank. 'I am in *so* much trouble,' she whispered.

Storm gave a sympathetic whine. 'It is all because of me. I am sorry, Madison.'

'It doesn't matter. I'd do the same thing again,' she whispered, just before her dad marched forward and stood in front of her with his hands on his hips.

'Whatever were you thinking of?' Mr Berry demanded crossly. 'I told you you weren't to come over here by yourself. Why didn't you wait for me?'

'I . . . I had to go after Storm. He ran off . . . because . . . um. He was scared . . . of something . . .' Madison began. She hung her head miserably as she realized that there was no way she could explain how desperate she'd been to find Storm, without giving away his secret.

'I'm sorry, Madison, but that's no excuse,' her dad snapped. 'You should have called me and we would have looked for Storm together. The way I see it, you ignored what I said, and deliberately ran off without me!'

Madison bit her lip. She knew that he was right in a way. There was nothing she could say in her defence.

Mr Berry sighed and ran a hand through his hair in exasperation. 'Well you can forget about that night watch!

We're going straight back home.'

'What? You're grounding me? You can't
. . . It's not fair . . .' Madison gasped, but
she could see by her dad's face that she
was wasting her time.

Mr Berry turned and marched towards
the street, obviously expecting her to
follow him. Madison had no choice. She
trudged after him, with Storm padding
along by her side.

'I don't suppose you've got any magical
ideas about how to get me out of this
mess, have you?' she whispered hopefully.

Storm shook his head. 'I am sorry,
Madison. Magic cannot solve everything.'

Madison nodded gloomily. 'I guess not.'

On their way to the house they saw
the Robertson's jeep pulling up. Madison
pulled a glum face at Ellie and drew one

finger across her throat to show that she was in deep trouble with her dad.

Ellie threw her a sympathetic look through the passenger window.

'I hope you find some dormice,' Madison called to her. *At least they won't have any trouble from those three boys*, she thought, cheering up a tiny bit as she thought of how Storm had taught them a lesson they wouldn't forget!

Chapter
TEN

Nanny Jen laughed and laughed when Madison told her about the night's events the next morning. Or at least, her own special version of things with all the magical bits about Storm missed out.

'I wish I'd seen those boys' faces when you threw grass and leaves all over them in the darkness. And the way you made ghost noises to frighten the little beasts too. That was quick thinking. You're quite a girl, Madison Berry!'

'Um . . . yeah,' Madison said looking sideways at Storm as she sprinkled a pinch of fish food into the tank.

Storm was curled up on the settee next to Nanny Jen. He woofed softly and wagged his tail to show that he didn't mind Madison taking all the credit.

'Anyway, Dad's calmed down now and I'm allowed to go over to the field with Storm when I get back from visiting you,' Madison added. 'So I'll be able to find out how Ellie and her dad got on last night.'

'Oh good.' Nanny Jen said. Her face changed as if she had something on her mind. 'I'd love to know what happened. Why don't you pop back here this afternoon and you can tell me all about it.'

'OK then,' Madison said, mildly surprised by her gran's sudden keen interest. Usually she was happy to wait until the next time Madison visited for any news.

'Don't forget now,' Nanny Jen said, wagging her finger.

Madison found herself wondering

if her gran might be feeling especially lonely. 'Nanny Jen was super-keen about us going back later, wasn't she?' she commented to Storm as they walked home.

Storm blinked up at her with wise bright-blue eyes. 'Perhaps she has a special reason.'

Madison frowned, wondering what Storm meant. She was about to ask him when they turned into her street. Storm saw Ellie taking something out of the jeep and bounded towards her.

The older girl spotted him and bent down to stroke him. 'Hi, Storm.' She stood up and smiled at Madison. 'Hi! I'm glad you're here. It's perfect timing. Come with me!'

While they hurried over to where

Oliver was up a ladder leaning against a tree, Ellie explained that they hadn't had much success with the night watch. 'We only found a few empty nests, like before. Dad was pretty disappointed as it's our last morning here, but then we noticed that there are nesting boxes in lots of the trees. We didn't see them before because they're quite high up and hidden by leaves. Dad reckons a local bird-lover must have put them up a while ago.'

'So they're supposed to be for birds?' Madison said.

Oliver looked down at her and grinned. 'Yes, but try telling the dormice that!' He got down from the ladder. 'You can go up and have a peep in this box, if you're careful.'

Madison's pulse quickened with

anticipation as she cautiously climbed the
ladder. Lifting the nest box lid, she peered
inside. She could see a cosy woven nest
and inside, curled up and fast asleep, were
three baby dormice.

The first she had ever seen!

Her eyes widened with wonder as she
took in their rounded ears, bushy tails
and dainty little pink paws. Their fur was
more grey than orange-brown and they
had long black whiskers.

After a few moments, she silently
closed the lid and climbed down.

Storm stood waiting for her, wagging
his tail. Madison bent down to stroke
him. 'Sorry I can't show them to you,'
she whispered. 'But I don't think Oliver
would be too keen on me taking you up
that ladder!'

Storm shrugged his furry little
shoulders. 'I do not mind. After all,
I cannot chase them like rabbits!' he
woofed cheekily.

Madison grinned at her little friend
and then turned back to Oliver. 'How

old are those babies and how come the mother dormice are using the nest boxes?'

'About three weeks old. The babies will be ready to leave in another week or so,' Oliver told her. 'The mothers obviously feel safer in the trees, because they don't get disturbed by people walking dogs and kids building dens and stuff. So far I've checked a dozen boxes and seven of them have babies in.'

'So it's official!' Madison said. 'This field's had a furry secret all this time and we didn't know it!'

Oliver laughed. 'That's one way of putting it. I've been in contact with the local wildlife trust and there's talk of making the field into a nature reserve.'

'Wow! That's fantastic!' Madison said. 'I saw a programme on TV about making a nature reserve. They needed lots of volunteers to help make paths and dig a pond and stuff.'

'Really?' Oliver said, his eyes twinkling. 'Do you know anyone who might be interested?'

'Definitely!' Madison said, beaming back at him.

After making plans to keep in touch with Ellie and Oliver, Madison took Storm for a good long walk and then popped home to tell her mum the amazing news before setting out for Nanny Jen's as promised.

Storm gambolled along beside her as they turned into her gran's street. They were just passing a small play area surrounded by bushes when Storm gave a whine of terror and shot towards the slide and swings.

Instantly alert this time, Madison heard a faint growling and snapping noise. She whipped round to see dark shapes looking into the front gardens a few houses away. Sunlight glinted on their pale eyes and extra-sharp teeth.

She gasped. Shadow's dogs! Storm was in terrible danger. The moment she had been dreading was here. Her heart pounded as she dashed into the little playground just as a bright flash of gold lit up the bushes behind the swings. Madison rushed forward and pushed through the branches.

Storm stood there, a tiny black-tan-and-white puppy no longer, but a majestic young silver-grey wolf with a glittering neck ruff. An older she-wolf

with a gentle face stood next to him.

Tears pricked Madison's eyes. 'Your
enemies are here! Save yourself, Storm!'
she burst out.

Storm's big midnight-blue eyes glowed
with affection. 'You have been a good
friend, Madison. Be of good heart,' he said
in a velvety growl.

'I'll never forget you, Storm,' Madison
said, her voice catching.

There was a final dazzling flash and a silent explosion of large gold sparks that sprinkled around Madison like fairy dust and which crackled as they went out. Storm and his mother faded and then were gone.

A furious snarling sounded at the entrance to the play area and then all was silent.

Madison stood there, stunned by how fast it had all happened. Her heart ached, but she was glad that she'd had a chance to say goodbye to her magical friend. She knew that she would always remember the adventure she had shared with him.

As Madison walked out of the play area, she looked up with tears in her eyes to see Nanny Jen standing at her gate, holding on to her walking frame. A young

woman stood next to her, holding a tiny
black-white-and-tan beagle puppy. There
was a van with an animal rescue sign on
the side parked nearby.

'Madison! I've got a surprise for you!
Come and meet my new puppy. I've
enjoyed having Storm around so much
that I couldn't resist. Especially as my
expert granddaughter has promised to
help me look after him!'

He even looks a bit like Storm, Madison
thought delightedly. So this was why her
gran had insisted that she come back for a
second visit.

'Here you are.' The woman handed her
the warm furry bundle. 'Your gran says
you can give him a name.'

Madison smiled down at the new
puppy as he gave a scared little whine.

There could never be another Storm, but she knew exactly what she was going to call this new friend. 'Hello, Magic,' she crooned, looking down into the puppy's melting brown eyes. 'You and I are going to get along *really* well!'

Out Now

A little puppy, a sprinkling of magic, a forever friend...

Magic Puppy

Spellbound at School

SUE BENTLEY

Spellbound at School

puffin.co.uk

Magic Ponies

A New Friend

A Special Wish

A Twinkle of Hooves

Showjumping Dreams

Seaside Summer

Riding Rescue

puffin.co.uk

If you like
Magic Puppy,
you'll love

A Summer Spell
9780141320144

Classroom Chaos
9780141320151

Star Dreams
9780141320168

Double Trouble
9780141320175

Moonlight Mischief
9780141321530

A Circus Wish
9780141321547

Sparkling Steps
9780141321554

A Glittering Gallop
9780141321561

Seaside Mystery
9780141321981

Firelight Friends
9780141321998

A Shimmering Splash
9780141322001

A Puzzle of Paws
9780141322018

A Christmas Surprise
9780141323237

Picture Perfect
9780141323480

A Splash of Forever
9780141323497

Win a Magic Puppy goody bag!

The evil wolf Shadow has ripped out part of Storm's
letter from his mother and hidden the words so that magic puppy
Storm can't find them.

Storm needs your help!

Two words have been hidden in secret bones in *Spellbound at School*
and *The Perfect Secret*. Find the hidden words and put them
together to complete the message from Storm's mother.
Send it in to us and each month we will put every correct message
in a draw and pick out one lucky winner, who will receive
a Magic Puppy gift – definitely worth barking about!

Send the hidden message, your name and address on a postcard to:
Magic Puppy Competition
Puffin Books
80 Strand
London WC2R 0RL
Good luck!

puffin.co.uk

It all started with a Scarecrow

Puffin is well over sixty years old.
Sounds ancient, doesn't it? But Puffin has never been
so lively. We're always on the lookout for the next big
idea, which is how it began all those years ago.

Penguin Books was a big idea from the mind of
a man called Allen Lane, who in 1935 invented
the quality paperback and changed the world.
**And from great Penguins, great Puffins grew,
changing the face of children's books forever.**

The first four Puffin Picture Books were hatched in 1940 and the
first Puffin story book featured a man with broomstick arms called
Worzel Gummidge. In 1967 Kaye Webb, Puffin Editor, started the
Puffin Club, promising to **'make children into readers'.**
She kept that promise and over 200,000 children became
devoted Puffineers through their quarterly installments of
Puffin Post, which is now back for a new generation.

Many years from now, we hope you'll look back and
remember Puffin with a smile. **No matter what your age
or what you're into, there's a Puffin for everyone.**
The possibilities are endless, but one thing is for sure:
whether it's a picture book or a paperback, a sticker book
or a hardback, **if it's got that little Puffin
on it – it's bound to be good.**